THE
MYSTERY
MANSION

THE
MYSTERY
MANSION

FORBIDDEN ARCHIVES

SAMIKSH SABIKHI

The Mystery Mansion
Samiksh Sabikhi

All rights reserved First Edition, 2022

© Samiksh Sabikhi, 2022

Requests for permission should be addressed to
authorsamiksh@gmail.com

To my parents for supporting me throughout this journey, my grand-parents and family for their blessings.

To the staff at Parkfield Primary School, London for helping me along the way.

A special mention for Mr Calvert, My Class Teacher who pushed me to take this work to its completion.

CONTENTS

Chapter One

Why was Sophia's Family so Rich? 1

Chapter Two

The Door at the End of the Hallway 7

Chapter Three

Of Age 13

Chapter Four

The Forbidden Archives 19

Chapter Five

The Eavesdrop 25

Chapter Six

The Wang Family Tree........................... 31

Chapter Seven

A Knock at the Door 37

Chapter Eight

The Fight Against Destruction 43

Chapter One

Why was Sophia's Family so Rich?

Sophia was a child born to amazingly wealthy and caring parents, Mr and Mrs Wang. She lived on the Greek island of Santorini in a mansion so big you needed a map to guide yourself around. It contained 373 rooms in total, most of which Sophia had never been in. The mansion was a place of mysteries. Her grandmother often told her stories of a pirate digging into the mansion and burying treasure in what they thought was a very smooth cave.

1

The Wang Family Mansion

You could find the most lavish bedrooms, each containing four-poster beds, engraved with rubies and gems of unfathomable value, these themselves could have lasted for one's lifetime. The studies had the most comfortable chairs, desks equipped with everything and a clerk, for some reason.

2

She was given everything her parents felt fit and was very well behaved and kind-hearted. She was also incredibly clever. She was the topper in her class at Euphort Wang Academy, a private school founded by her great-grandfather Euphort Wang. I believe you would be wondering: how did

her family get so rich from a private school? Well, they didn't.

The Wang family riches were passed down for centuries starting with Argus Bruxo, a merchant who sold ice cream at cheap prices. It cost a lot those days to make ice cream, mainly because you had to bring along ice blocks from long distances, as without them the ice cream melted – this was the only way to make ice cream. He overcame this expense because his brother, Aret Bruxo, agreed to bring ice for free as, bar Argus, the Bruxo family lived in the Village of Trastor in the tundra. This made Argus a great deal of gold coins, starting the family off.

After this, the family got richer and richer, eventually becoming to the present family, the Wangs.

Chapter Two

The Door at the End of the Hallway

The Euphort Wang Academy

It was the end of another day at school. Sophia was walking to the entrance of the building when she saw a door at the end of the hallway beside her. Usually, it was just a dead-end. She was a very curious girl and wanted to find out what was behind the door, so she decided to go towards that door instead.

Suddenly, the door vanished and out came an ordinary brick wall, not a sign of difference. She still walked to the place the door should've been in and it instantaneously appeared again, spruce planks with greasy metal hinges. "Am I hallucinating?" she thought. She opened the door…

Suddenly, Sophia was blinded. Light was seeping through the crystal panes on the side of a passageway. After adjusting her eyes, in front of her was an elegant passageway, lined with polished oak tiles and a glassy quartz floor. She walked into the passage, entranced by its mystifying air.

After walking for a few minutes, she stumbled across a magnificent, circular hall. It had a polished granite floor and the circular wall was embroidered with carved patterns and lined with spruce doors and signs.

She walked around and read all the signs. The signs were the names of places. The door she came through said 'Euphort Wang Academy' and others said things like: 'Santorini Stadium', 'Wang Industries', 'Wang automobiles', etc. She found a door named 'Wang House', which was what people called Sophia's home.

She went through this passageway, the same mystifying air filling it, and there came a button. She pressed it and suddenly the wall slid sideways. It led to the library at her house, as the bookshelf slid back. She walked out, confused and excited.

We have secret passageways leading to everywhere in Santorini! How could her dad hide this from her? She knew her dad knew about these passageways because he often appeared after a day at the office in the library without any evidence of coming through the doors. She never really thought about this but now she had the answer.

Chapter Three

Of Age

The Wang Mansion Party Hall

Sophia went to the entrance of the library, her parents... Her parents! Wearing silk, ornately sewn and comfortable clothes, holding shopping bags. She was going pale; she had never done anything without asking her parents or teacher. She had to be in great trouble.

To her surprise, her parents were smiling at her. They led her to the same passageway she came from. During that time not a word was spoken.

"This... This is the Wang family masterpiece," her dad announced. "This was made by Eupheme

Bruxo-Wang, only child and daughter of Aston Bruxo and Luisa Bruxo-Alvs. It has been expanded and updated ever since."

Sophia was at a loss for words, "You are thinking why I know you came from the passageway? Well, the Wang family has a gift, a gift of sorcery. This passageway was concealed with enchantments so that only a person who holds the ties of being a part or close relative of the Wang family can see it when they're of age of course." Her dad continued, "Since it is your twelfth birthday, you are finally of age and your sorcery powers are unlocked. Remember one thing, we only use our powers for good.

Also, you don't need to practice. Just think of what you want and it happens. Oh, I almost forgot, it's celebration time!"

Sophia was baffled by all this. It was like she had been whisked out of reality. She had read books with magical people in them, like Harry Potter, and it had always been thrilling for them after. "Am I in a dream?" she thought. She had always wondered how it would be like to be magical and now she was going to have first-hand experience!

The family went to the central hall of the passageway system and walked through the

door labelled Wang Party Hall. Her mom had made the cake and food, while her dad, demonstrating some magic, summoned lots of board games, movie discs and multiplayer console games.

Chapter Four

The Forbidden Archives

The Door to the Forbidden Archives

Sophia felt satisfied as she, over the following days, explored the tunnel systems after school. She knew now where all the entrances led to and ended but one. This door was a wooden door with rusted metal hinges, unlike all the grand decorative doors in the tunnel system. This door was entered through the secret Wang library. She went to sleep deciding she would explore that door the next day…

She was dreaming about the door.

Sophia opened this door and went inside…

It was pitch black. No light button in sight. Only the strange woosh could be heard through the blackness…

Suddenly, there was a little speck of light in the distance that kept getting bigger and bigger by the second. **"AAAAAAAAAAAHH!"** Sophia squealed as a foreboding figure emerged in front of her. "How dare you!" the figure whispered. Sophia, as pale as a light bulb, slammed the door shut and fainted…

Sophia heard a faint voice saying, "Oh, oh no." She opened her eyes and in front of her were her father and mother. Her father, seeing her

21

eyes open, unexpectedly said, clearly relieved, "Are… Are you OK?"

Sophia said in a shaky voice, "No, I dreamt…"

"I know, I know," said her dad and continued, "you dreamt about the door, the door to the Forbidden Archives."

Sophia stammered, "What…!"

Her dad abruptly interrupted, "The Archives are a place in the passageway that… That is Forbidden because they contain a secret, the secret to the destruction of the world. They were locked by my great grandmother's father,

22

but have been opened again… by someone in this…"

"Sam! Enough! She has heard enough!" exclaimed her mother, realizing something and growing white.

"Yes, yes she has," replied her father, now pale himself.

Sophia's mother got Sophia breakfast and hurried off with Sophia's father to what Sophia believed was the study.

CHAPTER FIVE

THE EAVESDROP

Sophia's Father's Study

Sophia's head was whirring with questions – What is happening? Are mother and father angry? Her face was still white and her light blonde hair were ruffled, unlike its beautifully combed previous form. Suddenly, a light bulb flickered in Sophia's head.

She started to creep to her cupboard, changed her clothes, combed her hair, and crept out of the room.

The hallway was as magnificent as it had always been like nothing had ever happened. The oak floor was glistening with cedar-panelled walls giving off a strong, flowery smell. She

crept up to her dad's study, relieved to see the clerk was not there. She crept up to the cedar door and opened it enough to hear the conversation.

"Sam, she'll be okay!" her mother said in a nervous voice,

"Bertha, the Runihura family has always tried to control children's dreams to open stuff using long-distance magic. Usually the Wangs tell our children not to fall for such tricks, but I forgot to!" her father said. "Don't you see? They could've found out much more last night than we know about."

"But then, but then, she… what should we do?" her mother said.

"We go and tell her what she needs to know," her father said, determined.

Sophia ran back to her room and sat at her table, worrying if her dad saw her. She took a minute to process this all when her mother and father knocked at the door. "Can I come in? I have to tell you something," her father said, forcing calmness.

Sophia let them in and her father started to speak.

"Are you okay?" asked her mother.

"Yes," Sophia answered.

"Were you wondering why we were so scared? Well, I have to tell you that if you ever have a dream like that try to wake up, never interact, okay?"

Sophia tried to pretend she didn't know a thing, "Why father?"

"One of our antecedents, Dysnomia Runihura, turned bad, the worst bad could go. She tried to rule the world with her intimidation and immense magical power but the good Bruxos

fought back and made her fail. Since then, she sought to destroy the world and to find the secret of how to do it. We locked up the book that contained the secret to the destruction of the world in the Forbidden Archives. Although Dysnomia is long since deceased, her goal is still sought-after by her present family, the Runihuras. They use the power of dreams to convince Wang children to unlock the Forbidden Archives using long-distance magic." Her father said, leaving him breathless. After that, not a word was spoken as the parents left the room.

CHAPTER SIX

THE WANG FAMILY TREE

Sophia's Study Desk

31

Sophia was feeling guilty about what she had caused. She had restless night after restless night thinking: What should I do to fix this? She tried looking for books about the Runihuras, but it turned out they had all been wiped off the catalogue.

She couldn't stand by her mistake and do nothing. Day after day she searched the majestic, red-carpeted floor with tall, stacked bookshelves with fibreglass sliding ladders. She could always find something using the computerized cataloguing but now even that was proving unhelpful.

This day water was sliding down Sophia's cheeks. Her eyes were red and her clothes hadn't changed for days. It was the most heart-breaking Christmas holiday she ever had. She was so muddled up with thoughts she had even started to pray.

She cleaned her face and started looking at bookshelf Z – the last one left to finish. She shuffled through the books Zodiacs and How to Beat Them, Zodiac Signs and The Wang Family Tree. "What?" Sophia thought out loud. This is in the wrong section. She slid it out and read the title, Wang Family Tree: Past To Present.

The Secret Wang Library

She quickly turned the pages until she found the chapter, 'Dysnomia, the worst a witch could go.' It was a short chapter that gave her the answer she had been looking for: Runihura Residence, otherwise unknown, is in the middle of the Bermuda triangle. The residence has been made unplottable because of this factor.

She then looked at the picture and imagined it moving outside the Bermuda triangle. Suddenly the address changed in the chapter, 'Runihura residence, before unplottable, is now located 500 hundred miles away from the coast in Florida', But now, another paragraph was written in the book 'Previously, the Runihuras

were trapped in the Bermuda triangle by the Wangs, but now are free because they have been freed by a Wang family member using long-distance magic.'

"Oh!" she exclaimed cupping her hand over her mouth. She had thought that by making the mansion plottable again, her father could take care of the Runihuras, not letting them destroy the world. But she had done the opposite…

CHAPTER SEVEN

A KNOCK AT THE DOOR

Door Knocker at the Wang Mansion

All that she had done was to cause destruction, opening the Forbidden Archives and freeing the Runihuras. She wanted to fix it all but couldn't trust herself. She started to read the secrets to defensive magic, and she had learnt a lot. She had used the spells she studied on a training dummy and had excelled in defensive magic considerably in the last few days.

She had to practice defensive magic because, although her father had told her to just think about it, it was for neutral spells. Otherwise the world would have not been here. She also got a wand from her father. "It needed to be made

after you were of age so you could channel your powers better," he had said.

She was very pale and scared these days. A Runihura could come out of nowhere now that she had freed them. She had also learnt that only the person who frees the Runihuras can fight them to understand what harm they inflicted on the other Wangs and people. "If only I had looked at another book!" she thought these days.

She went to her bedroom and laid down in her soft Saatva mattress, even if it did make her feel like floating in the clouds. It didn't make her any happier.

CRACK, BANG

KNOCK, KNOCK, KNOCK...

KNOCK, KNOCK, KNOCK...

She wondered why her parents didn't get it. So she got out of the room and cupped her hand around her mouth. Her parents were lying on the oak floor, looking lifeless. The floor was cracked, and the cedar walls were swiftly crackling with dust falling through the cracks. "We are alive... J-just stunned, only you can fight him now..."

The front door blasted open. Within seconds, Sophia put a shield charm on her parents to stop spells hitting them and ran back. In the middle of the debris and cracked wood stood a towering, foreboding figure, the same she had seen in her dream…

CHAPTER EIGHT

THE FIGHT AGAINST DESTRUCTION

"**V**olida!" shouted the figure. A giant mass of orange, red and yellow burst out the end of the figure's wand. **"Nerompala,"** Sophia blurted out. The raging fireball went out in smoke. **"Koepmy."** All the broken wood and sawdust swirled and sped towards the figure.

The Forbidden Archives

"Astima!" the figure shouted. The wood and sawdust crumbled and fell to the ground. "You're good, but not as good as me, **Seismos!"** The ground cracked under Sophia and she fell into the secret Wang library. The door to the Forbidden Archives lied in front of her.

"Well, you fool, I must offer greatest thanks to you for freeing me, but now is the time for my fight's reward," the figure continued, "to exterminate the Wangs! But before that…" He opened the door to the archives, **"Emfanzifos!"** A light came to the tip of his wand.

45

Inside, there was a cramped room filled with books. In the middle of the room, a book was floating – The Darkest Spells by Vincenta Goliath Rosenbloom. The figure swiped the book and looked inside.

Sophia crawled to her wand, her face bleeding and her arm bruised. **"Elenka,"** she whispered. Suddenly, all the books from the shelves in the Forbidden Archives bolt to the figure. Sophia stood up and shouted, **"Volida."** All the books lit on fire. **"NEROMPALA!"** All the books fell to the floor, soggy and burnt.

"You dare to fight me? **Chitypima!**"Sophia was knocked back onto one of the bookshelves. The remaining books toppled down. **"Gravata."** Ropes tied Sophia's body, tightening at the minute. **"Lyno,"** she gasped. The ropes untied and she fell to the floor.

"Looks like it's time for me to do the honours of destroying the world," the figure flipped the pages of the book. **"Volvata,"** she rasped. A rope on fire zoomed towards the figure's hands, burning his wand and wrapping him. **"Nerompala,"** Sophia said and the fire smothered. She snatched the book and lit it on fire. It fell down, becoming ash.

"Well, kill me then. Don't make the mistakes the ancient Bruxos made by showing mercy. Learn, my dear girl, and kill me." The figure said softly. "Say the words to the killing curse. It's right there under you," he pointed to the book's remains.

"No," she said, "You will be taken care of the Wang way." She waved her wand and a metal cage encased the Runihura. **"Episkevi!"** Everything was put back to the way Sophia wanted it. Books were fixed and stacked on the shelves, the secrets of destruction destroyed, and the Forbidden Archives gave another use – to store the remaining Runihura.

She also healed all the wounds and cuts on her body. She looked at the exit to the library and started to walk towards it. Suddenly, it opened. In the doorway stood her father and mother, beaming at her. "You know, I could never have done what you pulled off in a month after learning that you are magical." Her dad ushered her out of the room.

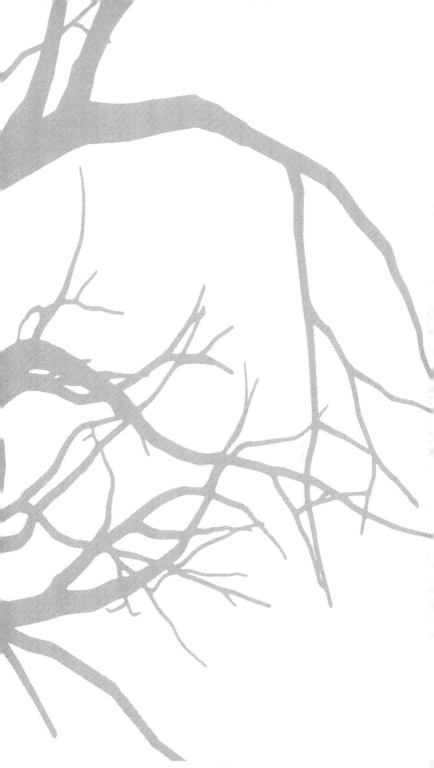